ENEMY ZONES

Andre Stewart
Enemy Zones

Published by BooxAI

ISBN: 978-965-578-153-3

ENEMY ZONES

ANDRE STEWART

CONTENTS

CHAPTER ONE

Roaring thunderstorms accompanied by rushing winds and heavy rains tormented the city of Montego Bay for hours. It was certainly not unusual yet totally unsuspecting as earlier in the day, the forecast was sunny, hot and the clear blue skies had no intention of producing rain. But as the sunset on the evening sky, and temperatures slowly fell, the heavens took the opportunity to fissure a gateway of rain, thunder and dramatic lightening. In Westgate Hills an affluent, upscale and sophisticated residential community, a chrome-black tinted 2014 Audi a4 sped through undisturbed. It was precisely 7 pm, but the night sky was pitch dark as if it was approaching midnight. The vehicle made its way along Miami Drive and then approached Queens Hill, where the driver pursued an unwinding uphill path until it pulled up to an exotic and exclusive playboy-like mansion at the top of Queens Hill overlooking St. James.

The vehicle was made welcome by steadily opening tall automatic archaic gates at the foot of the house and after it entered the compound, the gates closed briskly. The driver parked outside of his garage exited the vehicle and made his way towards the doorway.

He was of medium height and built of white complexion. Before his fingertips could even skim the door knob it swooped open in a flash and took him by surprise. A short, thick, big-breasted, dark chocolate mistress stood at the entrance covered in nothing but a pink bathrobe and flip-flops.

I've been waiting for you. She whispered temptingly in his left ear.

It was his hot 27 year old wife, Vanessa.

Their lips swapped to his arousal as her fingers smoothly loosened his tie and wrapped it around her neck with the tail of it in the palm of his hands.

I wonder what has gotten into you. He snuggled on her quivering lips.

His breath stanched of Cuban cigars and Hennessy while his plain white shirt oozed Mexican cologne. All this just turned her on more and more.

"Say…" he paused as he managed to get a sentence while tugging her lips with his before he continued. "Why don't you go upstairs and we'll continue this in the bedroom?" he posed.

His voice was diligent, smooth and sexy, some true attributes of a successful businessman. And his words only added more fuel to the fire that burned inside of her.

"Ok.. But don't keep me waiting." She said as she slowly walked away from him and made her way to the upstairs bedroom.

He watched every inch of her curvaceous brown body as she went up the stairs until he could see her no more. Even though the night was cool, he was sweating quite shamefully. He took his shirt off, exposing his bare chest and went into the kitchen for two wine glasses and a refrigerated bottle of champagne. From where he stood, he realized that the front door had not been closed and his briefcase had not been put up. He immediately put the wine bottles on the kitchen counter, put his briefcase on the living room couch and stared curiously out the front door as if someone was watching him secretively.

He then closed the door hesitantly and went to the upstairs bedroom to accompany his young wife, where they made sweet love into the wee hours of the morning.

At roughly 3:30 am, the showers ceased, but the breeze blew kindly enough to make the temperatures cool.

More champagne, sweetie? 'She inquired as she held the two half-drunken glasses of wine to his attention.

Sure thing, babe. He answered. Then she left the room to fulfill his request.

Meanwhile, he was at ease, relaxed and exhausted. He lay on his back, both arms behind his head and his eyes paced to the ceiling.

His mind was as calm and free-flowing like the beach on a sunny day and he let out a huge sigh as his eyes slowly closed

Bash! The sound of broken glass made its way from the kitchen to the upstairs bedroom, but he paid it no mind.

"Aaaaaaahi"

But now, the innocence of her voice surged into a terrified shriek, jolted him out of his comfort almost instantly. He pulled out his drawer and reached for his licensed black semiautomatic pistol and slithered cautiously down the staircase.

Bam!

He turned sharply from the staircase and faced the kitchen expecting an intruder in his house but saw no one but only the broken pieces of wine bottles he had heard from upstairs. He bent to pick it up and examined it carefully.

"Vanessa honey, is everything alright?" His voice echoed in the silence.

"Oh, it's not her you should be worried about." A familiar voice alerted him from the living room. His body jumped in fear and his head swayed madly, trying to match the sound of the voice with its direction. It seemed to have been coming from the living room.

That section of the house was dark and vague, so with outstretched arms latched onto his weapon, he approached slowly, with every step reluctant and fragile. Then suddenly, the lights flickered on and everything became vivid to him. He was about to shoot but he knew who the intruder was.

"Michael, what the hell are you doing in my house!" he exclaimed.

"Is that how you deal with business partners now?" The intruder said, a little amused.

He was a tail, handsome man of brown complexion dressed in a black three piece suit and tie.

"And besides..." he continued, "You know why I'm here. You have something that belongs to me."

He had a bottle of chardonnay in hand, which he poured out into a wine glass, then pulled out a chair and sat down, looking at the timid man pointing his weapon at him, but he knew that he wasn't going to shoot.

"Where's my money, Hugo?" Michael thrashed.

"I'll get you your money" Hugo fired back as he gripped his weapon harder than before, as if any minute now, he was about to shoot.

But Michael was calm, probably a good example of someone who has a great sense of humility. He sipped some of the champagne he had poured out, put the glass on the kitchen counter and stared Hugo dead in his eyes.

""It's been two years."

"Uh.." Hugo stuttered, "I need more time."

There was a moment of silence before Michael continued.

"I'm afraid you've ran out of time." He said, leaning forward.

Their eyes lost connection as Michael drifted his towards the small antique clock on the wall and back at him again. This caused him to glance also and the sight of his wife's head diced off her body and plastered neatly in the clock frightened his spirit.

"You son of a bitch!" He shouted in rage.

Click! Click! Click! His fingers exercised the trigger, but he had no bullets. He could feel his death now as Michael gave him a cold look and every part of his body shivered.

"What do you take me for?" Michael questioned him. As if he wasn't already shaken up. So he feared to even answer.

"Deal with him, Jasper" Michael said calmly

And out of the shadows, a 6'10 figure appeared and covered Hugo's mouth and stabbed him mercilessly as Michael watched, sipping champagne unmoved. When he seemed to have stopped fighting his fate, Jasper stopped. Michael then rose from his seat, drew for his silencer and hammered him 5 times in the head.

Pow! Pow! Pow! Pow! Pow!

After the gruesome act, he drank the rest of the champagne, dropped the glass on the kitchen floor and both men left the house.

Later that day, numerous detectives pondered on the scene to examine the evidence, but the professionals managed to disconnect themselves from the act.

CHAPTER TWO

"Vroom!"

A red-tinted Mercedes S Class pulled to the entrance of a 12,000 sq ft mansion built in the hills of Montego Point On the inside, two tall, fully bearded and muscular security guards armed with deadly force approached the vehicle cautiously. By the time they reached the driver's side, the window swindled down slowly, revealing the cool and subtle face of Michael Sanchez.

"Tell Charles its Michael, he's expecting me,"

The men then stepped away, radioed their boss and alerted him of the arrival of his visitor. Then after a few seconds, the gates were opened and Michael proceeded into the compound untroubled, The synthetic building had a touch of elegance and class, poise and complete luxury. Security cameras were everywhere and you simply could not browse freely without passing a guard.

Meanwhile, after cruising past the entrance, Michael parked beside a fashionable figure fountain of Hercules and Pegasus with water squirting out of the horse's mouth. The car was turned off and he made his way to the balcony of the top floor to Charles Nicholson; a billionaire businessman and his partner in crime.

"Ah yes, Michael!" he greeted him favorably.

The guards that escorted Michael up the flight of stairs then left and he alone stood facing the Man.

"Take a seat." He followed.

The balcony of his house edged over all the other properties in the hills of Montego Point while being a front-row seat to the Caribbean Sea, Champagne on ice was set out on the table for their evening discussion, which was in progress. "My sources have given me new information about you." Charles said.

Instead of partaking in drinking the champagne that was designated for him, he reached for a cigar from his top pocket and a lighter.

"Do you mind?" he asked before he ignited the tobacco.

"Of course not." Charles calmly reassured.

"What have you heard?" Michael asked as he lit the cigar and blew the combustion from his nostrils and mouth.

"Nothing of great significance." He said sarcastically.

"Your words." Michael said coolly, trying to dismiss the topic completely.

"Listen…" Michael finally added. "We are men of high status and standards; we can't afford to have ANYBODY owing such small sums for so long and not paying them back. I don't regret my actions; Hugo had to pay his debts one way or the other." he strongly emphasized.

Michael knew that Charles had an idea of the killing but he tried to shift the topic to something of greater importance.

"Shipments are going great." He said "But even though we haven't got caught in the act as yet, I think we should up our game or sooner or later we will get caught and I'll be damned if all the tracks lead to us." Michael finished.

With their great chemistry and position of power in Jamaica, the trafficking of drugs seemed easier but actually posed more risks.

Michael was the Mayor of Montego Bay, St. James and Charles a filthy rich businessman. Through his millions, it was possible for Michael to even attain certain possessions and could even have been elected as Mayor for so many years. So in some cases, Michael could not have the last say but being good friends, they had a great understanding of each other.

Later that evening, both men were connected to an Italian drug lord that lived in the States through a telephone call. He went by the nickname 'Carlos' and the three men were discussing a possible international transaction between two countries.

"This is a risky move; we don't want any holes in our baskets."

Everything must go as planned. Carlos demanded at the other end of the telephone line.

The afternoon disappeared as the evening was made welcome by cool temperatures and the bright setting sun. The balcony where the men lounged was fused with smoke after Michael burned cigar after cigar.

"So it's settled..." Carlos said "A private jet will land at Boscobel on New Year's Eve with the exact amount of 'stuff' that we agreed on. 100 kilos, no more no less." A pause followed his sentence before he momentarily continued his speech.

"If everything works out as planned on our side, you will hear from me within 3-5 working days. If not, do not try to contact me." His words were sharp and they pierced like a knife.

"Is everything understood?" he questioned.

"Every word." Michael said confidently

"Perfect! Then you will hear from me very soon…"

CHAPTER THREE

New Year's Eve 2k15

Numerous persons flocked to the streets all around the island, charmed in an atmosphere of pandemonium and excitement as they greeted the New Year with joyful celebration. On the Eastern end of the island, though is where some serious action was about to take place. No matter what power Michael had attained through his position in the game of drugs, no respect was shown to authority.

The country was geographically set up with 14 parishes, 3 counties and two main sections, East and West. Michael and Charles shared all the territory in the West, and the East was controlled by their enemy 'Tyreke'. And even though everything was planned and orchestrated before time, it still seemed like a recipe for disaster.

It was early in the evening, but nightfall was steadily approaching. A collection of 2 black shaded Range Rovers and 2 pickup trucks parked just below the runway after shortly arriving at the secluded destination. A small army of dangerous gunmen assembled from 'The West Empire', stepped out of the vehicles; their weapons tightly grasped in their hands as they waited for the arrival of their boss.

In no time, the notorious red-tinted Mercedes drifted violently through the airstrip before it came to a halt and parked stylishly ahead of all the vehicles. Jasper, Michael and Charles; three of the most dangerous men from the West disembarked from the vehicle.

"Alright men!" Charles shouted. "Let's get down to business!" Wham! Wham! Both trucks were lifted open and the ganja, which was stashed in strong Ziplock bags, was removed one by one from the trucks. But in the middle of their hustle, a picturesque small aircraft departing from the night sky caught their attention and they stopped what they were doing to watch it land smoothly.

It was a black, custom-designed, leather interior 737. After positioning itself perfectly on the runway, in front of their patient acquaintances, the door steadily opened. One minute passed, two minutes passed, three minutes passed and still nobody had left the aircraft since it landed. Time just seemed to have frozen.

"What the hell is this, Michael?" Charles murmured under his breath.

"Just stand your ground." Michael said sharply. No one had considered moving a muscle.

Then finally, the tension was relieved when two armed men came out of the plane and stood by the door weaving a path for Carlos to exit.

"Gentlemen…" he said, approaching both Michael and Charles slowly.

He was short, a little over 5'5, had crisp black curly hair, white complexion and his rigid accent gave him off easily as an outsider.

Both men approached him and greeted him professionally by shaking his hand. A smirk appeared on Charles's face as he found it amusing how this man is respected as a gangster when he was so short in stature. It made him wonder. But he kept a lid on his emotions and tried to be professional.

The men continued unloading the sealed packs of weed from the trucks onto the small plane and finished soon afterwards. "100Kilos?" Carlos asked sternly.

"Not an ounce more or less." Michael said reassuringly.

Carlos then turned away from both men and signaled to one of his bodyguards, that stood at the doors, to retrieve something in the plane. He went in and returned with three briefcases and presented them to Carlos, who then delivered them to the hands of Michael.

"5 million?" Michael inquired as he took the briefcases and peered into them one by one.

"Not a penny more." Carlos bloated.

"Perfect!" Michael replied. "I hope to hear from you very soon."

Both men shook hands and were about to take off in separate directions.

CHAPTER FOUR

When the transaction had been completed, both parties set out to part ways. The jet had been ignited and ready for takeoff when both parties shared their final remarks. However, camouflaged by a scheme of forest trees and bushes, a secret onlooker watched from a distance. His car was black-shaded and with the vagueness of the night, easily undetectable. Along with that, he was of dark complexion, medium height and very slim. His loyalty was with the East Empire, where they identified him as 'Jake'. He was not particularly proficient, but the ability to trail your enemy and spy on them for such a long time while remaining hidden was a pretty neat asset.

In no time, the small aircraft rapturously embodied the night sky as Carlos and his team departed the island. But before the men on the ground left the 'private location' Michael suggested taking a different route back to the west. Firstly, the money was shared amongst his colleagues as promised before. Then they were split up into groups of two; one group traveled on the southwest of the island whiles the other traveled on the north coast.

Jake, who was seated in his car examining every little move being made the entire time, thought it'd be in his best interest to leave before his foes realized that they had an uninvited guest.

Vvvr! Vvvr! Vvvr!

He lodged the key into the ignition, but the car failed to start.

"Come on! Come on!" he said, panicking.

His hands fidgeted on the car keys as he tried to kick start the engine but the results returned negative. To make matters worse, his car blocked the exit and entrance, which was a one-way. The heat of the night terminated the cool air as he began to perspire nervously when his eyes glanced at the collage of vehicles approaching his direction. He needed to find a way to deliver himself out of this situation and he needed to find one fast!

He tried a few more times to start his vehicle, but it was still unresponsive to his request. If only he had known that this would be the outcome, then without a doubt, he wouldn't have put himself in this position, to begin with. But what could he have done now to fix an already messed up situation?

He began to gaze nervously around his environment, maybe he could've hidden himself smartly amongst the trees, bushes and plants until his enemies had left. But the physical characteristics of his surroundings didn't guarantee complete security; however, the fear for his own life was enough to make him reconsider that idea. And he was rather feisty in his endeavors where he managed to hide between the frames of two tall mango trees.

"That should do it." He murmured confidently to himself.

He tried to adjust his stance firmly on the grass and have his upper body lean against the trees to reassure himself that he was completely hidden from plain sight. Now, all that he had to do was to stand still, keep his composure and make no subtle movements whatsoever.

Bash! Bash! Bash!

The departure of the team played right on cue and no sympathy was shown to the dysfunctional car that barricaded the exit.

Broken glass, a cracked windshield and slammed doors were the circumstantial results after one of the trucks surged violently into its side. The arrival of the other vehicles came momentarily and the mysterious vehicle was the center of everyone's attention.

"We've been spied on." Michael said softly while staring seriously faced at the crushed motor vehicle.

His mind began to race and shift on a million ideas all at once, and then he focused his vision fiercely on the innocent looking bushes and trees.

"Scorch them!" he ordered, pointing at the bushes in the direction of Jake. "Whoever was there still is!" He added.

A man from the scene then reached for a tall bottle of kerosene he dug up in the trunk of his vehicle and damped the bushes as ordered. Michael stood anxiously as he watched to see what would become of it. It was as if he alone could've sensed in his spirit that the presence of someone was very near, and he was about to find out.

Woosh!

The bushes were set ablaze and a small fire quickly grew into a big flame; spreading by the seconds. Along with it, a clustered cloud of smoke emerged and the fire also brightened the scene, making objects close and far away appear less vague. With the crackling sound of wood, and leaves being burnt, Jake sneakily aborted from his position and slipped deeper into the bushes, hoping to feel another way out.

He trudged and trudged and trudged till he came to a complete stop after real-izing that he had been on a cliff and there was really no room more room to escape. He stood at the edge staring over the cliff and across at all the city lights in Kingston and the tough and pointed rocks that posed below him. It was as if he was right back where he all started, and he would've needed to strategize another method to escape all over again.

Then suddenly, the rush of movement through the bushes approaching his direction alerted his senses. With no space to hide this time around, he reached for his pocket knife and stood his ground, ready to defend himself from who or what may appear.

The sound came closer and closer until he was standing face-to-face with the boss himself.

"I knew I smelt something fishy around here!" Michael said coarsely as he looked at the man with vicious intentions. His gun was gripped at arm's length and loaded with dozens of bullets just waiting to be activated. Time seemed to have frozen as both men stared at the other with disgust.

"Little boy, what are you doing showing up at badman place!"

Michael continued.

"Last time I checked, this is our territory?" Jake answered back fearlessly. There was a moment of silence before he continued.

"It was you who stepped out a line. Know your place!" he grumbled.

Even though Michael was much older than he was by a couple of years, Jake put him on notice to let him know that he was just as tough and bad and that his little antics would not be tolerated with him. Their eye connection was broken as Michael looked at the pocket knife he had grasped tightly in his hand by his side.

"Watch it man! You're nothing but a camouflage, real badman don't bring knife at gun war?" He riddled.

"Then drop it and fight like a man." Jake insisted.

The night was subtle as the air grew thick almost instantly.

Bam! Michael dropped his weapon slowly, but it fell heavily on the grass and in the blink of an eye, Jake swung his blade at him ruthlessly. Michael sighed in his attempt and used his strength to haul him on his back and tried to retrieve the pistol he dropped on the grass. But in his efforts Jake wheeled his leg at him and Michael fell on his back, nearing the edge of the cliff. He took a while to get back on his feet, but Jake was already up and he began to choke Michael with all his might.

The showdown between the two men was fast and exciting like it would've taken place in the movies.

"Look at what you brought upon yourself; you shouldn't have trouble what don't trouble you. Now you're going to die a dreadful death." He muttered as he choked Michael aggressively.

For a man so skinny, he was surprisingly strong and Michael found it hard to overpower his resistance.

Pow!

Almost nearing unconsciousness, Michael struggled, but in the midst of it all he managed to retrieve the fallen pistol and fired a bullet into the man's backside, who yielded loudly in gruesome pain. But he was not dead yet. Michael scuffed through his pocket reached for the man's phone, snapped a picture of his wounded body and forwarded it to all the contacts in Jake's phone.

"Let me tell you this..." he said, standing up and looking down at the ailing man with triumph in his heart. His words were smooth, precise and of complete dominance.

"Never underestimate the heart of a real gangster."

Jake's cell phone was thrown over a cliff and splattered in fine pieces amongst the rocks after the picture of his wounded body was sent to everyone who knew him.

"For as long as your momma lives, she or no one else will find your body." Michael spoke hauntingly.

Wham! Just one blow to the hip and his body went sailing over the cliff.

"Aaaaah!"

His screams of terror were so loud and desperate it was really unfortunate that no one could hear them and come to his rescue. But it didn't help midway through as the loud and colorful fireworks ignited towards the night sky, which signaled the start of a new year.

CHAPTER FIVE

As the year settled in, the horrific image of Jake's body began to surface. It was the main headline on the 7:00 news and in big imprints in the local paper.

"Picture of dead gang member Darrell 'Jake' Williams circulates on social media."

Everybody and their mothers knew about the dead man, but still his body could not have been found.

St. John's, Antigua and Barbuda

A bright, sunny day descended on the nation's capital with hot and humid temperatures enrolled in its arsenal. Just a few hours of private airtime was enough to transport Michael from his native Jamaica to his luxurious summer home in the mountains of Antigua, where all that really mattered were daytime adventures and bedtime stories.

Splash! Splash! Splash! Splash!

Stroke after a stroke made the water blurb as Michael watched his 11-year-old son Miguel propel his slender body from one end of the pool to the other in a series of effortless blows.

"Did you see that, dad? Did you see? Did you see?" Miguel beamed gleefully as he stopped to take a breather.

"Did you see how fast I was going and the way I flipped my arms?" he puzzled as he motioned his arms in demonstration.

"Hey man, you were amazing." Michael said, giving him a high five.

"But you gotta stock up some more pounds; you know what I'm saying?" he joked while playfully elbowing his slim body.

"Yeah, I know what you're saying man. But you gotta promise to lose some pounds to!" Miguel replied, chuckling while he shadow-boxed his father's stomach. And they both laughed.

He loved his son, there was no doubt about it; the young lad was his pride and joy. He cherished the time he spent with him, which was really not that often, to begin with as work and family relations were separated from each other and rightfully so too. The further away, the better. A child should not grow up in a negative environment and in one that poses a threat to their life. But someday, he hoped to retire to spend time with his son and sulk up in his millions, far from the life he would've lived in the present and in the past. The telephone rang in the pool house, which was nearby and he was about to get it.

"Hey man, I've gotta take this, but how about you get dried up and we go get some ice cream later?" Michael asked, much to the delight of Miguel, who cheerfully agreed. And he did just that.

"Hello..." Michael said as he answered the telephone.

"Hey Mike, it's Charles." The caller identified, and before Michael could've interjected, he continued.

"We need to talk; we've got a big problem on our hands." The man spoke softly and suited his words with a sense of concern and sympathy, so instantly Michael knew that something had transpired back home.

Not totally alarmed at the breaking story but still interested in the nature of it all, Michael took a seat before he continued.

"What happened?" he asked.

"We've been attacked! This time it's brutal. We've lost a great number of our men and some innocent civilians are dead. All eyes and ears are on you and the media are hungry for a story to sell." His words were soft-spoken and stroked with a sense of urgency and concern, but still, that was the last thing Michael would've wanted to hear. Instantly his imagination began to produce some possible scenarios to picture it all up, and he began to worry a little.

"Michael, you there?" Charles beckoned as moments had passed without a reply.

"Michael... Michael." He continued to call out.

Michael held the phone firmly in his hand but still contributed to the silence as his mind wondered on a million things all at once.

"C'mon man, you've gotta talk to me." Charles said.

Probably that sentence brought him back to reality, and he prepared to conjure up a sentence or two.

"So they wanna attack us, huh...?" Michael said seemingly.

"Roll out the army, my jet is going to be fueling up; I'm coming home."

CHAPTER SIX

V.C. Bird International Airport, St. John's Antigua
Two days later

A slight breeze hassled about the busy airport as it prepared every. One for the main event, which seemed to be light showers and a theatre of lightning. Accompanied by his baby mother, his son and his personal colleague Jasper, Michael was getting ready to leave the country headed for Montego Bay. His private jet had been refueled and ready for takeoff as soon as he stepped onboard, but he was in no rush.

"Hey man." He spoke softly to his son as he tried to stoop down to him when he spoke.

"I had a really great time with you the other day but I have to go now."

"Okay!" Miguel murmured distastefully. His eyes flooded with water while he dressed a frown, obviously displeased with the news."C'mon man, no tears?" Michael said as he hugged him, trying to soothe his discomforted spirits. Good-byes are never easy, he thought.

"I promise I'll be back in time to spend the summer with you." He continued.

"Until then, just keep working on your freestyles and we'll see if you're good enough to beat me!"

A big smirk appeared on the young lad's face as Michael smiled with him too.

"See ya later, pal." He finally added, patting him on the shoulder and rubbing the waterworks from his eyes.

He shared his final goodbyes with his family before boarding the plane, which took off shortly afterwards.

Montego Bay, St. James

After being in the air for almost two hours now, the flight came to an end when the aircraft landed smoothly at the Donald Sangster International Airport. Rich or poor, the procedures remain the same; the passengers had to be screened by security and pass through customs and immigration like any other person traveling. But after that mandatory process was completed, Michael encountered a media-crazed audience who impeded his personal space just to get feedback from him. Flashing lights and video cameras with a sea of news reporters firing question after question about the recent attacks on their city. It was literally impossible for him to walk through the airport in one piece.

"Mr. Mayor, how do you plan to approach this crisis?" one female reporter asked.

"How do you think this is going to affect your votes for this year's election?" Another questioned.

The rally went on and on, sparing from different categories, but Michael chose a firm decision and opted not to respond to any of them. If he had spoken, he knew in his mind already what the outcome would have been. All they would've done was to turn and twist his words against him for their benefit to be negatively publicized and he was not up for that.

After successfully maneuvering his way through news reporters and camera crew, he was within a few steps from his chauffeur, a tinted 2015 Chevrolet van. His suitcase was applied to the trunk and he and Jasper drove away from the airport, leaving a trail of media house representatives behind.

Later that day

A scene of smoke flowed from the balcony of Charles's mansion as the men smoked joint after joint while engaging in harmless small talk that lasted for hours. The day was finally over, drawing to a close with 40 minutes left before midnight. It was a relatively short day. Traveling back home took up most of the day and when they got back home, it was back to business. Michael lived a life of pure complexity but made it seem effortless. Maybe his secret lied in his ability to hire a network of persons to do all the work on his behalf and report back to him with all the necessary information. Certainly, that was how he did it. Being Mayor of one of the largest parishes in the country, he would have an assistant mayor in his office doing all the paperwork, making the calls, but at the end of the day, Michael would be the one to speak at press conferences (which he seldom did and clamp down on serious decisions when necessary). All that strenuous work and the irony of it all is people swear that they make 7-8 figures when they actually don't.

That opens up an avenue for his other 'profession' as a drug dealer which accumulates wealthy sums. But in that area, he is more hands-on and practical than before.

The money is made in an interesting variety of channels. Firstly, when the weed is harvested, it is sold by 'ground men' in the streets and on hotel beaches and clubs to tourists along with other drugs like cocaine, heroin etc. But when it is not sold in hotels or clubs, it is snuck onto cargo ships heading to the US and UK, where it manages to get onto the streets of London, Birmingham, Miami, and South Beach. With this method, the dealers are more likely to get caught but it nets a cool income of 10 million for each crate that gets through successfully. It worked out well for a while until both countries began to launch an investigation into the whole matter, which led to the arrest of a large number of corrupt international officials; the drug market crashed. That was three years ago. It is one of the more vivid and fresh memories in Michael's mind because, during that time, he was staring bankruptcy right in its face. He lost his investments in real estate, as he couldn't pay property taxes and other outstanding bills.

He started loaning money out to be paid back at relatively slim interest rates while trading some of his valuable possessions for cash. But even that didn't materialize as how he'd hope it to. That was truly a dark time in his life; he couldn't make ends meet to sustain his businesses and provide for his family, all while being a target for execution by his enemies. But in due time, he rose above that and overcame his struggles.

It is true what they say then; things get worse before they eventually get better. These days Michael spends his time stacking up enough millions to retire but still runs the game of drug dealing by being the chief supervisor of ganja shipments going abroad.

Things are not easier, but rather, his approach to all his responsibilities differed from before. He is more serious-minded, lucrative and has better control of his temperament.

But at the present moment, he was relaxed. All that projected on his mind was how he was going to handle tomorrow's events.

CHAPTER SEVEN

The Next Day

Bright lights and attentive faces decorated The Montego Bay Conference Centre, where the Mayor of the parish, Michael Sanchez, is scheduled to address the public in the presence of news reporters and media representatives who budgeted their time to broadcast his every word. It was Friday afternoon: the weekend was no longer creeping up but instead presented itself with clear blue skies and cool temperatures. The birds sang in harmony as they gushed through the brave wind and soared above the subtle seas.

Even though Michael was not too fond of speaking with the media, he arrived early to deliver his messages and plans for his constituency. He showed up sleekly in his red Mercedes vehicle, accommodated with his assistant Mr. Pryce. No entourage or bodyguard tugged along with him today. Their time and energies would be reserved for something of greater importance.

"Good afternoon, ladies and gentlemen." Michael said as he made his opening statements.

"The past few days have been dreadful, terrifying and an unbearable experience for all Jamaicans." He spoke.

"The news of the attack on our city that stole the lives of so many innocent civilians and injured many others saddened my heart." When he finished that sentence, he issued a pause before he spoke again and he could hear the glittering whispers and flashing camera lights that echoed around the room.

"The cry for the cease of crime and violence in our nation has been a difficult transition, but with the help of God Almighty, the battle will continue because we will not let criminals and infidels have their way in Jamaica land we love." The whispering congress turned into an applauding audience as they seemed to be moved by his continuing presentation.

Eastbound-Kingston

Eeeerks!

The sizzling smell of burning rubber from car tires rose to the atmosphere. Jasper and Charles, along with the remainder of the gunmen that survived an attack on their lives just days before, were grouped in an avalanche of vehicles packed with explosives and ammunition. The skyline setting in Kingston was quite similar to that in St. James, but the bumper-to-bumper traffic on the major roadways and highways in the capital city differentiated the two. However, the sizable army split through the chaos and confusion as they privately schemed through the community of Norbrook, where they pounced upon a gated (3) Story home secured by pit bulls and a few security guards.

Pow! Pow! Pow!

No time was wasted; as the mob appeared on the scene, they blasted several gunshots at the guards, who dropped dead. Automatically, the dogs began to bark but were wounded to silence by tranquilizers. The main gate was forced open and some of the men rushed in while a greater handful stayed behind to secure the perimeter just in case the cops came.

The property boasted seven bedrooms, a guest house and a lengthy pool you could spot from the entrance. It was a sight to see!

But the team was not here to splurge on the amenities of the house.

Bam! Bam! One by one, the doors in the house were knocked down and the rooms scrutinized in search of Tyreke, the don of the East.

So far they split up and by doing so, went through 5 rooms and now 2 remained. Certainly, he must've been in one of the two. The team regrouped and prepared to fire as they slowly opened one of the two doors.

Screech!

The door tweaked open imperceptibly and when it did, they came to the realization that no one was there. One room was left and it lied at the top right-hand corner of the house, but some of the men were already in disbelief and a little too dispirited to even consider checking there; but they did so anyways. They climbed up the stairs, browsed through the hallway and midway through they were showered by vast amounts of gunshots.

Pow! Pow! Pow! Pow! Powl

The shots rummaged wildly about the hallway but failed at meeting any human targets. However, throughout the attack, a glimpse of a tall, muscular figure escaping from the room greeted their eyes. It was Tyreke. A short, light-skinned girl eluded from the bedroom too, screaming while trying to hold a white towel to obligate her nakedness. But she was still noticed. Tyreke was shirtless but rocked blue-cut jeans as his heavily inked body glistened in the sunlight. He locked a small Beretta handgun which aided him in his escape as he hurdled over the balcony and lofted neatly onto the grass, where he took off like a jet. Most of the men were caught with their guards down, but Jasper eluded the staircase and was in hot pursuit of Tyreke's trail. And instantly, some of the other men followed too.

"Dammit! Josh, one of the two remaining men on the scene," said.

He had not run off but stood looking over the balcony at Jasper chasing Tyreke.

"C'mon, let's go!" he exclaimed to Max, another man on the scene next to him.

Josh aimed to run off in Jasper's assistance, but Max stayed back; something had grasped his interest which caused him not to run off like the others had done. He knelt down and in the pinnacle of his hands and in between his fingertips laced a 20 carat gold chain belonging to Tyreke, which valued millions. Its beauty sparkled in his eyes and he secretly stashed it in his pocket and then ran off.

Bam! Bam! Bam! Bam!

Gunshots hammered while footsteps plastered about the big yard as the heated chase after Tyreke played on. Even though his property was quite big, sooner or he was going to run out of real estate.

But for now, he had a slight advantage against his foes. His sprinting form was top-notch as he dashed across his backyard, heading towards his guesthouse, which was a small building that lied next to a brick wall fencing his house from his neighbor's. Almost acrobatically, he managed to climb on top of it and launch himself over the wall and next door. But he failed to get a clean escape as 3-4 bullets purged his upper body and one gazed at him in his calf muscle.

Pow! Pow! Powl Pow!

Now you would think that would've been enough to kill him, but Tyreke continued pacing because he literally knew that his life was on the line, Jasper, who was the first to trail him, nearly caught up with him but thought he would've been dead when he got shot multiple times and was very surprised to see the man climb a 10 foot wall! Jasper's mind, protested the idea of breaching the wall to finish the job and kill Tyreke but was discouraged by the scream of sirens approaching his direction. That caused him to restructure his focus to disappear from the scene, which he and everyone else managed to do.

Later that day

After dispersing from enemy zones earlier today, the survivors of The West Empire franchised a route back to their original enterprise, where they gave the boss a complete rundown of how things went.

"See what we thief from the boy here, boss!" Max said, presenting the expensive gold chain to him.

Michael didn't gravitate much to the idea of Tyreke surviving his planned attacks, but on the other hand, he couldn't find himself being disappointed and somewhat ungrateful in the eyes of his posies. He held the gold chain high in the palm of his hands, with his comrades around watching attentively. How pleasing it would've been to know that his enemy's existence was one for the history books, he thought to himself.

CHAPTER EIGHT

One Week Later

The morning presented light showers and a cool weather front as Mid-March captured the attention of every calendar in town with January and February long gone. The local government elections were right around the corner and all the candidates took to the streets and inner city communities to persuade people to vote for them this coming election. Social media, TV ads, radio broadcast, and flyers. Everything was used at their disposal to reach out to their desired audience.

For decades, the two major political parties in Jamaica were the JLP (Jamaica Labor Party) and PNP (People's National Party). And, of course, there was a struggling party that ran against the two heavyweight contenders that didn't materialize any real voter profits to grant them any major power in the country. That party was the NNM (The New National Movement). It had only 20 members and Michael was actually their most successful candidate.

Being elected Mayor back to back for 2 years in a row, he was seeking to be in office for another year. Ironically that was one of the places he could rarely be found, but today was an exception.

The building that served as his office was a small studio located in downtown Montego Bay on Glendevon Avenue. This morning he and everyone in the NM party were there as they met to disclose their plans to ensure achievable results this year-round.

The meeting lasted nearly an hour, a relatively short duration and when the meeting ended, the members' interest was in leaving.

Michael was in the midst of the departing party, talking with the others as he moved along the hallway to the exit. When everyone from the political congregation left the building, some of them started their vehicles and departed right away, while a few others stayed back in the parking lot, sharing a discussion with each other. Michael facilitated their conversations to his interest but was about to cut his sentences short when he noticed that he had left the keys to his Mercedes behind in his office. He excused himself for a short while, turned round and approached the main door of the office to retrieve it.

Bap! Bap! Bap! Bap! Not even a split second had passed and gunshots were aimed wildly in his direction. However, the drive-by attack was short and amateur as nobody got hurt, but some of the brave motor vehicles that were parked suffered some minor injuries like cracked windshields and headlights, while some had punctured tires. It caught everyone off guard. No one got a real opportunity to visualize the perpetrators in the act, because it occurred so quickly and most persons ducked beside their cars for safety.

"But is what the rahtid this brethren?" A Rastafarian member of the party expelled shell shocked!

The others around reacted in astonishment as fear swooped through their bodies.

Now, Michael was not hurt or terrified but came to the assistance of those who seemed to be a little traumatized and tried to calm them down.

"Are you alright?" he calmly asked a young lady that hid at the side of her van but fell to the ground. He held her hand to draw her up off the ground and to let her stand on her own two feet, while picking up her belongings. Someone on the scene dialed the police, who gave their word that they would arrive soon. But Michael and some others were not too keen on being present when the police arrived and so they left.

3 hours later

After leaving his office downtown, he drove to Charles's house, which was built 3 blocks away from his. Jasper was also there too, and both men welcomed Michael's presence with alcoholic beverages.

The men were all seated on the balcony of the top floor, across from a framed view of the beautiful Caribbean Sea. There they were engaged in an era of discussion with Michael contributing to a larger share of the conversation.

"Me a tell you, as me turn to go get me keys." Blam! Blam! Blam!

Around 4 shots, the boy then let go after us and drove off, he recalled today's incident.

"Eee, so the thing set now?" Charles jumped in.

"Yeah." Michael confirmed.

"You all should've made sure that boy died the other day or we wouldn't have to deal with this!" He added with an upset mood and tone of voice.

"We did what we could." Jasper said firmly as he looked over to Michael, who sat on a brown sofa beside Charles.

"Yeah... He managed to jump over the balcony, wall and fence after we shot him 3 times!" Charles spoke surprised as he retold Michael of Tyreke's lucky escape a week before when they came to murder him.

"It's alright man! I know what him want to go down!" Michael said calmly. "Is me him want to bait up to come down there to fight a war me can't win." He added. "But any day name day I come to town for him, it's going to be problematic on his shoulders."

Just as Michael finished that sentence, Charles's phone rang and he took it out of his pocket to answer it.

"Hello..." he said.

"Boss!" one of the security guards that worked at the main gate to his house called out through his phone.

"Yes!" Charles answered.

"You've got company." The man said.

"Really... Well, who is it?" Charles asked.

"It's the police and they're here to take you all in custody."

CHAPTER NINE

A couple of police officers accompanied by a search party from the JCF (Jamaica Constabulary Force) all parked outside Charles's mansion, flashing their blue lights as they stood hosting their fire. Arms screw faced. The two security guards at the opening gates of the house granted the law enforcers a permit of entrance into the building after the warrants were presented to them and they fully understood the situation at hand. After which, 3 pairs of police vehicles which included the search team, drove into the residence.

Now, when the news of the police arrival reached the men, their little time of peace and relaxation ran out and they tried to create for themselves extra time to hide some of the dozens of firearms they had lying around the big house; but would they be lucky enough to get away with it?

"Good morning sir, what seems to be the problem here?" Charles beckoned as he asked one of the senior police officers who now stood face to face with him downstairs.

"Good morning sir, my name is Mr. Delroy Atkinson from the Westmoreland Division, and we have a warrant to search your property for illegal firearms in

"

connection with a shooting that occurred on the 21st of February in the vicinity of Norbrook." He stated professionally.

And while they spoke downstairs, Michael and Jasper were upstairs stashing away anything that'd be considered illegal privately in the attic, before they too made their way downstairs.

"What shooting?" Charles asked.

"On that day, the 21 of February..." the senior inspector began to explain. "Some reports were made to the St. Andrew police by citizens who claimed to have seen a group of men in that area when the incident occurred..."

"So what does that have to do with me?" Charles said as he interrupted Mr. Atkinson midway into the ending of his sentences. The man was a little annoyed, but his response didn't reflect his actual mood.

"Well if you must know..." he continued.

"When we investigated further into the matter, we received CCTV and surveillance footage from video cameras in that area, and you were spotted along with a couple of other men on the scene, some of which we currently have in custody!"

That was news to his ears, and after Mr. Atkinson had finished speaking, Charles stood calmly; his hands rested in his pockets as he didn't utter a word. Guilt had taken him over. When the officer realized this, a devilish smirk appeared on his face and he thought to himself how easy a bait Charles was.

"Mr. Sanchez..." The officer called out to Michael, who now stood directly beside Jasper and Charles after leaving upstairs a few seconds ago.

"Yes sir." Michael confirmed.

"May I ask what you are doing here?" Mr. Atkinson said.

"Well, these are very good friends of mine and I'm here paying them a visit." Michael said, turning to both his colleagues he stood beside.

"Oh?" Mr. Atkinson said softly.

"Well, you'd be interested to know that both your 'pals' are considered prime suspects in a shooting incident that took place earlier this month and will be held in custody for questioning."

"Oh really..." Michael said slowly as he gave the man a cold hard look, a look that implied and reflected his ferocious and sadistic thoughts.

"I had no knowledge about that." He added.

"Mmmhmm." The officer misted under his breath. A crazed idea entered his mind at the same time but he chose not to disclose it.

"Well we've got video evidence on them both, so I doubt the judge would grant them bail..." The officer said coolly. "Anyways," he continued loudly. "These officers are here to search the building for any illegal firearms or ammunition that you may have around the house."

After Mr. Atkinson finished his sentences, he instructed the officers who made up the search party to ransack and turn the whole house upside down until they found a gun or anything they would consider illegal, to slap charges on the men.

An hour had transpired and the officers were still in the big house, carefully searching the property room by room. It had been 12 minutes past midday and the sun was in peak performance.

While the majority of the officers were all about the house, the 3 men sat at the front desk, talking to each other in hushed tones.

"Then is how much of our boys Babylon hold on to, and how comes is that police boy there make us know what's going on?" Charles muttered a little furiously.

"Is that me would like to know too. How the man them don't let us know what's going on?"

Michael responded.

"Yow, something was going on man?" Charles said.

"Boss." Jasper said as he was about to break the silence he upheld within himself.

"You know that the other day when we left Kingston, some argument did occur between a few of our soldiers them and it looked like it was going to get serious before I intervened and calmed them both down. And after that day passed, I haven't communicated with either of them. I don't even know if they're dead or alive."

"Perhaps one of them got arrested and they gave out our whereabouts!" Charles added after Jasper finished talking.

"Right now, it doesn't matter how the police located us, our main concern should be destroying that piece of evidence that they have against us before it reaches the courts."

Michael couldn't make any more sense and his counterparts agreed with his prepositions. And before anyone of the 3 'suspects' could release another sentence, they were alerted of the presence of Mr. Atkinson, who held a black pistol in a Ziploc bag pressed within his fingertips. More police officers flocked out of the building too soon afterwards. It was as if they had found what they'd been looking for.

"Mr. Nicholson... Does this weapon belong to you?" Mr. Atkinson asked,

"Yes, that's mine." Charles replied.

"Well, do you have any documents to show that it is a licensed firearm?"

The question was dished out into the open air awaiting a response, but it took a while to be served on the receiving end. A plague of silence flustered about as the officer looked down at Charles, who had his eyes on the parked police cars that posed beside his fountain. In his mind, different thoughts rallied about based on the present, future and past.

"I'm not answering any further questions without my lawyer present." He finally responded.

"I see..." Mr. Atkinson jumped to say.

He then passed the firearm he held to a 'squaddie' who stood beside him and reached for his handcuffs that rested on his backside.

"Well, we'd still have to take you into custody."

What he said was clearly understood and the instruction was simple. Jasper and Charles stood up, were searched by other surrounding officers and cuffed to be taken away. Once that was done, the two detainees were escorted to a police van parked adjacent to the main door, where they sat in the backseat. That was not an easy sight to see for Michael, who sat on the more comfortable chairs of the deck easily and unrestrained. He knew that something had to be done to ensure that they wouldn't be 'victimized' by the situation as soon as possible.

At approximately 35 minutes after 1, a dark cumulus cloud brochure across the city of Negril as the bright, shining sun was nowhere to be found. However, the day progressed rather quickly as the security officer was about to leave the mansion, accosted by both suspects.

The sirens were activated while the engines roared loudly when the police made their exit, leaving a trail of exhaust behind from their mufflers. And as for Mr. Atkinson, he was gone with the others too. He did what he came to do and left without saying a word to Michael. But Michael didn't leave the house immediately after they did. He boarded the flight back up the staircase, where he lounged on the comfy balcony sofas, drinking, and smoking all by himself. He did this for a great deal of the day and when nightfall approached, he drove intoxicated back to his house 3 blocks away, where sleep was the first and only thing on his agenda.

CHAPTER TEN

The next day

After yesterday's events deeply subsided into the history books, the challenges of a new day arose. With time campaigning against his liking, Michael's main priorities were completing his important objectives. Today, daylight had captured him in his office downtown, even though he locked himself away in isolation, the sun's rays just simply crept through the window curtain.

However, his attention was centered on his computer screen while he held discussions over the telephone business-like connection he acquainted himself with in his early days.

"Ok, Marsh… I'm on the website now, what should I do next?" Michael said.

"Sweet! Now look for the section that says member's login area at the top right-hand corner of your screen." Marshall said.

Michael listened to his instruction and moved the cursor in the direction specified.

"Mmmhm…" he muttered.

"Alright, now type in 'All 42' in the username and seventeen-hundred as the password." Marshall continued.

"All 42 and seventeen-hundred…" Michael repeated.

"That's right." The man confirmed.

He did just that and before his eyes flashed, an analytics show of pie charts, line graphs and up-to-the-minute stock prices coated in red and blue colors in front of a neutral background.

"What's all this man, some sort of programmed network or something?" Michael asked.

Marshall chuckled on the other end of the telephone line.

Meanwhile, Michael was in the process of deleting tabs from his web browser when the clatter of boots pounding on the tiled floor stopped and a soft knock pelted on his door.

"This is the police, Open up the door!"

The knock on the wooden door persisted again but this time, Michael opened the door knowing in the back of his mind that he would regret ever doing so afterward. And he actually did so sooner than he thought.

At the door, the old yet familiar face of the senior inspector from yesterday secured a perfect position in Michael's eyes.

"Yes, sir." Michael said softly.

The office was awfully quiet.

"Mr. Sanchez." The inspector said gingerly.

His response reflected his facial expression, wretched and disgusting.

"Based on our investigations and research with what we collected at the station, we need to take you into custody for further questioning on the whole matter. We feel you might know more than we think you do." The inspector said.

His red crushed lips scripted the words professionally, but his tone of voice portrayed otherwise.

"What makes you think so?" Michael asked, annoyed.

"Well, you know both witnesses very well." The officer said.

"But that still proves nothing" Michael said childishly.

"Yes. But our purpose still stands, you're gonna have to come with us."

No matter how vile and savage those words sounded, they were quite accurate. The doors to the office were closed as handcuffs were sealed onto Michael's hands.

He trudged through the hallway, his cuffed hands resting in front of him as a number of officers surrounded him when he walked.

Their movements were rapid and lively and in no time, they all reached the exit. His secretary, Simone, was astonished and left speechless when she saw Michael walking away in shackles. The two made no interaction whatsoever. She just simply sat around her desk, looking at him as he passed and he held his head straight, as if she didn't exist. Perhaps he felt a little too awkward and ashamed of himself. Whereas outside, a small crowd of passers-by, probably 5-6 persons, stood watching their Mayor being accosted by the police. Their presence simply could not have been ignored. Even though all along they watched quietly, when Michael sat in the backseat of the police's car some whispers could be heard.

Inside the vehicle, Michael sat screw-faced with the sun seeping through the clear window beating on his smooth brown skin.

Bam!

One of the squaddies that led Michael into the vehicle, slammed the door loudly on purpose, then walked away with a smirk on his face. However that didn't faze the detainee who sat in the backseat untroubled. If anything, his nerves were calmed, but his sense of resentment was far from being kindled. Anyways, the sirens were activated and the police vehicles raved away from Park Avenue.

**The Police Department
Barnett Street, Montego Bay.
A Little Later In the Day**

From his comfy office sofa to the slim iron chairs in the interrogation room, a cloud of frustration followed him. His thoughts were not free flowing as before and that credits to him being in a place of restriction and not one of freedom and luxury he creates for himself. And up until this day, he proudly held a police record; he has never been arrested, charged or found guilty of any illegal activities. That complements him nicely in the eyes of the public, but behind curtains and closed doors, his dealings are unprecedented.

Screech!

After being led into the interrogation room to sit for a while, the senior inspector, Mr. Atkinson, came in and sat on the opposite end facing Michael. He carried with him a file jacket containing some documents and his reading glasses. He put on his glasses, opened the files and scripted through the documents one by one. Michael watched him keenly until he stopped searching and took up a thin paperclip document.

"So… Mr. Sanchez. Mind telling me where you know Mr. Nicholson and Mr. Richards from?"

Mr. Atkinson said, looking at Michael through the lens of his glasses.

"He was a friend of mine in high school?" Michael simply said.

"Is that so…" Mr. Atkinson responded.

"Yes…"

"What high school did you attend?" Mr. Atkinson then asked.

"Meadowbrook."

When Michael spoke, Mr. Atkinson took a pen and wrote all his responses on a fresh notepad.

"So what kind of work does Mr. Richards do?"

"He is my personal assistant." Michael said

"But that's not what he told me when I questioned him."

That is indeed what Jasper said to the man when he was interrogated, but Mr. Atkinson chose to tell a blatant lie! Michael was puzzled at this, but his outer characteristics did not show it.

"Ok" he said.

"And Mr. Nicholson, what does he do for a living?" The inspector asked.

"He is an entrepreneur."

"What business does he own and operate?" Mr. Atkinson asked.

"I don't know, why don't you ask him?" Michael said.

"You've been friends with him since high school; certainly, he must've shared aspects of his occupation." Mr. Atkinson implied.

"Well he and his business are his concerns, not mine!"

A short moment of silence echoed in the room as both men looked at the other dead in the face. A turbulence of tension was slowly rising.

"Ok, fine. Well, do you know these persons?"

Mr. Atkinson held up some mug shots of faces Michael is familiar with, which are really members of his gang.

"Yes, I've seen those faces before."

"Fine, but do you know these persons." Mr. Atkinson said.

"I'm not answering that question without my lawyer present. Next question." Michael said roughly.

"Well then, are you prepared to remain in custody until he gets here?"

Michael had no answer for the old man, their eyes just made four with moments of silence just passing by.

"Do I need to repeat myself? Because it seemed as if you haven't registered the question I asked." Mr. Atkinson said.

"Don't need to."

Michael's response was cheap and insolent and it pissed the inspector off.

"Alright, fine. You've already decided and you make it bad on your part..."

No more meaningless utterances or lines of conversation was needed; Mr. Atkinson just ordered Michael to stand up and have some officer nearby escort him to an empty jail cell and from the interrogation room.

"Put him in isolation." Mr. Atkinson said evilly to a nearby squad die who gripped the cuffs on Michael's wrist.

"Yes sah!" The officer answered his senior.

'Isolation' was referred to as a desolate area on the compound where small jail cells were built to temporarily house inmates who could pose a dangerous threat to the department by having a strong influence on fellow inmates who will follow their orders like a boss or don. Already having the knowledge that there are a couple of inmates present in Michael's contacts under lockdown, the police instantly made sure that he had no connections with them while there.

Those cells are much smaller and without windows or a proper 'lighting system'. The inmates there are allowed merely 30 minutes a day of recess and aren't permitted to see visiting friends or family members. There is no TV, radio or any means of entertainment, just a bed, toilet and sink. Anyone who has ever experienced 'Isolation' can tell that it is a reality of a nightmare, and that was where Michael was heading to.

Three police officers walked with him through the compound to the specified location, and once the cell was opened there was no turning back.

"Get comfortable man!" One of the officers who made the journey with Michael told him humorously. What he said captured a sense of irony and as he walked away, he topped it all off with an evil laugh that echoed and faded through the building. There was no comfort here for Michael to indulge in, instead he was humbly in the fortress of the law.

CHAPTER ELEVEN

Seventy-two long, uncomfortable and unpromising hours terminated. Out of all his 'linkies' Michael was the last to get incarcerated but the first to be let off on bail. Jasper and Charles were more serious attributes though and the force chose not to grant them any free-dom. For both of them, it proved to be a sticky situation, but fortunately for the 'man at the helm' of it all, his lawyer ruled in on his case and all suspicions were dropped. But not all was smooth sailing. Because of his incarceration, voters lost confidence in him which caused him to lose his position as Mayor in the parish of St. James. And with his jailed crew, their whole team suffered a huge injury. Who's to tell? The whole money-making scheme of drug trafficking could end prematurely.

"Mr. Sanchez, Mr. Sanchez! Mr. Sanchez! What a familiar situation."

Guarding voices and flashing camera lights with microphones and recorders ready to tape the words of the ex-mayor, Michael Sanchez. Probably 72 hours behind bars was not enough to pres. Sure the man and the media came to play their role. His Mercedes was right around the corner in the parking lot to rescue him from the venue if he could just manage a couple more steps. So far, he held his composure as his lawyer walked with him along the way, and as he trudged through, it seemed as if he would be home free.

But a bright and brave cameraman who moved with Michael suddenly pushed the lens of his camera up close to Michael's cheeks rudely.

"Get that shit out of my face!" Michael exclaimed.

He brushed the video camera from his face and the short cameraman fell to the floor with his equipment taking the fall with him.

The others took a step back but videoed continuously as the Mercedes skirted away. No doubt in anyone's mind, that that would've made the headline news at 7.

Nightfall

The community of Negril Point rested in silence. There was nobody's house to go to, because none of his friends were around to drink, smoke and talk to, so Michael could be found on the patio of his own house all by himself. It was 10:30 in the night and he was down to his last bottle of Hennessy; he had been drinking heavily since the start of that evening. Where did it all go wrong? How could he fix it and make things right again? What would it take to get the job done?

Drunken thoughts swayed just as the slight breeze swished through the night air. Michael was not certain of what to do next, but he knew that something had to be done.